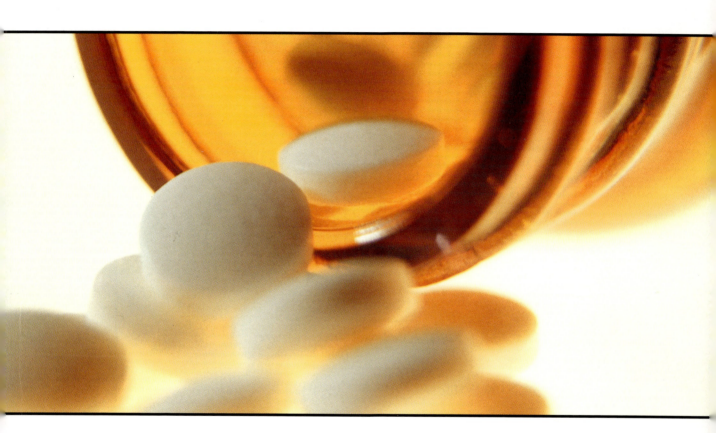

SUBSTANCE USE AND ABUSE

UNDERSTANDING GLOBAL ISSUES

Introduction

The United Nations (UN) estimates that the global trade in illegal drugs is worth more than $300 billion per year. This trade accounts for eight percent of all international trade. Production, **trafficking**, and abuse of synthetic drugs is increasing around the world.

More than 95 million Americans over age 12 have tried marijuana at least once, making it the most frequently used illegal drug in the United States. Nearly ten percent of teenagers in the United States and Great Britain admit to having used cocaine at least once, and 1.6 percent of American eighth-graders admit to using heroin.

The United States sets the tone for drug control policies around the world. In the United States, marijuana, heroin, and lysergic acid diethylamide (LSD) are classified as Schedule I drugs. These drugs are considered to have very high abuse potential and no accepted medical use. Schedule II drugs, such as **amphetamines**, **barbiturates**, cocaine, codeine, and morphine also have very high abuse potential, but may be prescribed

▬▬ **On International Day Against Drug Abuse and Illicit Trafficking in 2005, Afghanistan burned nearly 60 tons (54 tonnes) of drugs, the world's largest illicit drug burning ever.**

by doctors in strictly controlled circumstances. Great Britain has similar rules. However, in February 2004, Great Britain reclassified **cannabis** from Class B, with amphetamines and codeine, to Class C. Under Class C rules, in most

Approximately 80 percent of all crime in the United States is related to drug or alcohol addiction.

cases, people in Great Britain caught with cannabis will not be arrested for possession of the drug.

There is no question that illicit drugs are harmful. However, the dangers from most illicit drugs are often exaggerated. For example, each year, tobacco, a legal drug, causes more than 440,000 deaths in the United States. Excessive alcohol consumption causes more than 100,000 deaths each year. Illicit drugs account for more than 19,000 deaths.

Studies of the long-term health effects of illicit drugs are complicated by inadequate data, changing fashions, variable content, and use of multiple drugs. Street drugs vary widely in strength and quality. The average purity of heroin and cocaine available in the United States has greatly increased since 1980, and stronger varieties of cannabis have become more widely available. Since all **psychoactive drugs** reach the brain, their long-term effects on cognitive function and personality are cause for concern.

Attitudes toward drugs vary with time and place. Societies adapt to drugs, soon dropping those that clearly cause harm. Regular use of illicit drugs falls markedly as young adults mature and take on family responsibilities. By contrast, about half of those who smoke cigarettes in their teenage years and 80 percent of alcohol users go on to acquire lifetime habits. The comparative rate for illicit drugs is 10–20 percent. Nicotine is more addictive than heroin or cocaine, but nicotine is legal. Social and legal attitudes toward drugs are full of paradoxes like these.

Why People Take Drugs

A cup of coffee is not the image that comes to mind when the subject of drugs arises. Most people associate the word "drug" with illegal street drugs. However, drug applies to a wide range of substances, including alcohol, caffeine, nicotine, and numerous medical products, as well as illegal drugs such as cannabis and cocaine.

Almost everyone takes some kind of drug. The main reason is to feel better, whether that means enhancing pleasure, improving performance, or easing pain. Drugs change the sensations carried by the central nervous system. For example, caffeine increases the heart rate, pumping more blood to the brain.

Drugs that increase social harmony are accepted more easily than those that bring private pleasure. Early coffee

---

Almost everyone takes some kind of drug. The main reason is to feel better.

---

houses, for example, were centers of brisk conversation and social interaction, combining cultural norms and a fashionable new drug—caffeine. A modern parallel is so-called "club drugs," which enhance the user's mood. Methylenedioxymethamphetamine (MDMA), or Ecstasy, is one such drug.

Drinking alcohol is a much older custom than that of drinking coffee. People have enjoyed the intoxicating effects of beer, wine, and spirits, or distilled liquor, for thousands of years. Societies across the world share the habit of drinking alcohol, though the varieties of alcohol consumed differ. The social convention of drinking alcohol is so ingrained that parents often offer their teenage children this

▰ Coffee beans can be processed to remove caffeine. However, a cup of decaffeinated coffee still contains about 3 mg of caffeine. Nearly one-third of the world's population consumes coffee. This is more than any other beverage.

psychoactive drug without a second thought. These same parents would never consider offering their children marijuana.

Inconsistencies in social attitudes to different psychoactive substances not only cause much debate and confusion, but also send mixed messages to youth. Societal attitudes toward drugs are formed more by fashion than by health impacts. Some drugs can and do cause much damage to health and society. Governments have a responsibility to protect citizens, but people also have a right to freedom of choice. It is sometimes difficult to achieve balance between the two. Education about the short- and long-term physical and mental impacts of different drugs is vital so that people can judge for themselves the risks involved. Education becomes even more important as drug use spreads to the **developing world**.

DRUGS AND THE BRAIN

Drugs affect the central nervous system and parts of the brain, giving the user feelings of pleasure. Some drugs reach the brain quicker than others. For example, eating or drinking provides a relatively slow effect because the drug must be absorbed through the digestive system. The first puff of a cigarette, however, delivers an almost instant nicotine kick to the brain. A drug sniffed up the nostrils or placed under the tongue also works quickly because absorption through mucous membranes is quicker than digestion or skin absorption. Some drugs work in the brain because they are similar shapes and sizes as natural neurotransmitters, which are natural chemicals made by nerve cells in the brain. Drugs lock into receptors in the brain and cause an unnatural chain reaction, causing the nerve cells to release large amounts of the drug's own neurotransmitters. Some drugs cause nerve cells to release more neurotransmitters or cause unnatural floods of neurotransmitters. Drugs that stimulate pleasure centers in the brain are especially addictive.

The Race to the Brain

All drugs of abuse create feelings of pleasure in users. Depending on the method of delivery, it takes longer for users of some drugs to feel pleasure than users of other drugs.

inhalation (smoke or gas)
5-10 **seconds**

intravenous injection
15-30 **seconds**

muscle or skin injection
3-5 **minutes**

sniffing up the nose (snorting)
3-5 **minutes**

mucous membrane contact
5-10 **minutes**

eating or drinking
20-30 **minutes**

KEY CONCEPTS

Central nervous system Psychoactive drugs affect the central nervous system, which is basically the spinal cord and the brain. The brain receives about 20 percent of the human body's blood flow. To counteract the potentially destabilizing impact of substances carried by the bloodstream, the brain's nerve cells are bathed in a fatty fluid that acts as a protective barrier. The ability to cross this blood–brain barrier is a key factor in the potency of a drug and the time it needs to take effect. Combinations of drugs may have unforeseen and potentially disastrous results, especially where they inhibit the life-support functions of the central nervous system, such as breathing.

Club drugs Fashionable drugs taken at all-night dance parties, such as raves, are referred to as club drugs. These drugs are often taken by young adults. Methamphetamine, LSD, and MDMA (Ecstasy) are among the most common club drugs.

Why People Take Drugs

The Social History of Drugs

Every society has its own drugs used for medicinal, religious, or recreational purposes, such as hemp in India, opium in China, coca in the Andes, and hashish in the Middle East. Human **physiology** impacts which recreational drugs a society accepts. For example, the digestive systems of Europeans are better at processing alcohol than those of indigenous North Americans or Asians.

In many parts of the world, beer and wine were safe drinks in times when clean water was a rare luxury. Beer and wine also made people forget the hardships of their daily lives. The spread of **distillation** methods not only made cheap spirits available to the masses, but also increased the social consequences of alcohol.

Vodka was used in 18th–century Russia to placate unruly subjects and gather revenue from **excise taxes**. In 18th–century Europe, gin consumption wreaked social havoc in urban areas. Governments responded to alcohol abuse by raising taxes and creating more regulations. Although the United States imposed **Prohibition** for a brief period, the cultural popularity of alcohol soon overcame official attempts to eradicate it.

Tobacco was imported from the Americas in the 16th century and rapidly established itself among European upper classes. Tobacco was used as snuff or in a powdered form. Although tobacco was widely used, it was only in the late 19th century that manufacturing techniques made cheap cigarettes

▬ **Prohibition began in the United States in 1919. Bootleggers sold alcohol illegally across the country.**

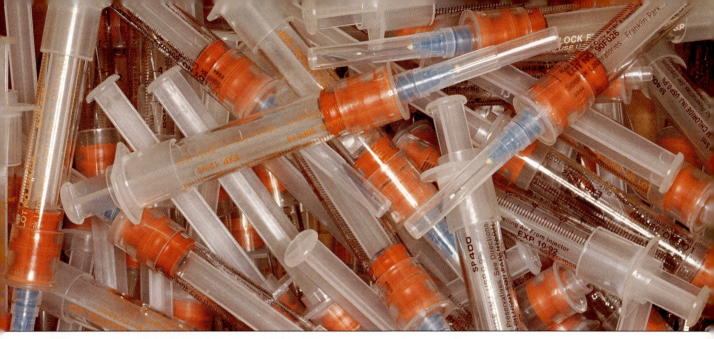

Alexander Wood invented the hypodermic syringe in 1853, which he used to inject patients with morphine as a painkiller.

available to the masses. By 1964, when the U.S. Surgeon General warned of the health dangers cigarettes posed, smoking had become almost universal in Europe and the United States.

The Industrial Revolution changed the social use of drugs. In addition to mass-produced cigarettes, the invention of the **hypodermic syringe**, the chemistry of separating the most psychoactive substances from plants, and the development of synthetic drugs in laboratories all played a part in increasing the potential for pleasure and abuse.

Coca has a long history. Archaeological evidence indicates coca was domesticated by 1,500 B.C. South Americans have chewed the leaf of the coca plant as far back as history records. Peasant Incas chewed coca to endure the hardships of daily life. It provided gentle stimulation. A wad of coca leaves mixed with lime from crushed seashells exuded a steady dose of cocaine in amounts sufficient enough to quell hunger pangs and fatigue but not strong enough to disturb physiological or psychological balance. Early

---

The Industrial Revolution changed the social use of drugs.

European invaders shipped the leaves back to their homelands, believing coca would benefit their societies. The coca leaves lost their potency on the journey; however, and coca had little effect on those who experimented with it. Europeans therefore soon lost interest.

Europeans rediscovered coca in the 19th century. Combinations such as Vin Mariani, a mixture of red wine and coca leaf extract, became popular energizing drinks in Europe. The medical profession—including Sigmund Freud—enthusiastically embraced cocaine. By the 1860s, it was regarded as a wonder drug that would cure many illnesses. Cocaine was widely used in medicinal tonics and toothache cures. It was used briefly as an ingredient in Coca-Cola™ in the late 19th century. Although coca leaves remain in the Coca-Cola™ recipe, cocaine has not been used in the drink since 1903. The cocaine content is separated and sold to the **pharmaceutical** industry.

The medical benefits of opium have been recognized for many centuries. In Great Britain, opium became a popular recreational drug in 19th-century middle-class society.

The Social History of Drugs

It was often taken with alcohol as a potion called laudanum. However, the habit of smoking opium was imported from China, creating numerous opium dens in the back streets of London. At this time, social attitudes to the drug began to change. In early 20th-century America, recreational opium use was banned by U.S. law.

Despite a long history of medical use, both opium and cocaine fell into disrepute in the early 20th century. Brisk sales of opium- and cocaine-based products led many people into addiction. Governments hurriedly introduced control regimes in response.

Other psychoactive substances have often been welcomed into polite society. British chemist Sir Humphry Davy, for example, introduced the recreational use of nitrous oxide, or laughing gas, into early 19th-century middle-class drawing rooms. In the 1960s, enthusiasm for psychedelic drugs such as LSD originated in American universities.

■ Opium can be extracted from the milky latex that excretes from an unripe poppy seedpod. Morphine and codeine can be derived from the poppy seedpod as well.

Psychedelic drugs produce changes in the user's perception or mood. Timothy Leary, a well-known U.S. author, lecturer, and psychologist, experimented with the such drugs and promoted their use.

The rise of pop music accompanied the fashion for mind-altering drugs. Jazz musicians in the 1930s used marijuana and cocaine, but the habit did not spread outside the entertainment industry. Rock

KEY CONCEPTS

Cannabis, hemp, and marijuana The terms cannabis, hemp, and marijuana often seem to be used interchangeably. However, they are different drugs derived from the same source. The hemp plant, native to Asia, is the source of marijuana and cannabis. Cannabis is the drug produced from the dried leaves and flowers of the hemp plant. It is smoked or chewed. Marijuana contains the dried flowers and leaves of the hemp plant. It is smoked or eaten as a drug.

Industrial Revolution The Industrial Revolution was a period when machines changed the way people worked and lived in many parts of the world. It began in Great Britain in the 1700s and spread throughout Europe and North America in the 1800s. The industrialization of manufacturing was the result of new technologies, such as power-driven machines, and new work methods, such as factory production.

Understanding Global Issues—Substance Use And Abuse

THE OPIUM WARS (1839–1842 AND 1856–1860)

As part of its expansionist trade strategy, the East India Company—strongly backed by the British government—was keen to sell goods to China. China, however, was uninterested in western ideas and products. China wanted to export tea but did not want to buy anything in exchange.

There was, however, demand among the Chinese population for the East India Company's opium. The company owned Indian plantations and had an abundance of opium. Although opium use was long-established in China, the practice of smoking it for pleasure was not widespread and was frowned upon by the authorities. Growing opium poppies in China was forbidden. To help balance its trading account, the East India Company began exporting opium to China in defiance of the law. Sales were strong, and a flourishing **black market** developed.

When Chinese authorities destroyed a large quantity of opium in 1839, Great Britain sent gunboats in response. After several years of war, limited trade was agreed upon. The trading limits were ignored, and the China tried to block their ports again. French naval forces joined British warships. China suffered humiliating defeat after the two opium wars. Chinese ports were opened to free trade with Great Britain, France, Russia, and the United States, and Hong Kong was leased to Great Britain until 1997.

China's system of government suffered as a result of the opium trade and wars. The British, however, did not view opium as merely a habit-forming and dangerous drug. Its medical uses were highly regarded, and laudanum was commonly used as a painkiller. Many public figures, including Florence Nightingale, took opium regularly. In outposts of the British empire, including India and Africa, opium was regarded as a reliable remedy for stomach upsets and tropical fevers.

bands of the 1960s—including the Beatles and the Doors—made drug use fashionable. Drug use became part of youth culture. Widespread drug-taking among Vietnam veterans who succumbed to the temporary relief of drugs reinforced widespread drug-taking, even though most soldiers who took heroin in Vietnam did not pursue the habit after returning to the United States.

Opium den A place where opium is sold and smoked and that has facilities for people to stay while they are under the drug's influence is called an opium den. An opium den usually has pillows or mats for users to recline on while the dreamlike, dissociative state the drug induces wears away.

Recreational drugs Drugs taken for pleasure or leisure are called recreational drugs. These drugs are rarely taken under the supervision of a physician. The term "recreational drugs" is often applied to MDMA (Ecstasy) and other drugs that are associated with raves, such as amphetamines and LSD. Some recreational drugs are addictive, may be harmful to the user's health, and are usually illegal. Recreational drug use implies drug use is part of an individual's lifestyle even though he or she may only use drugs occasionally.

The Social History of Drugs

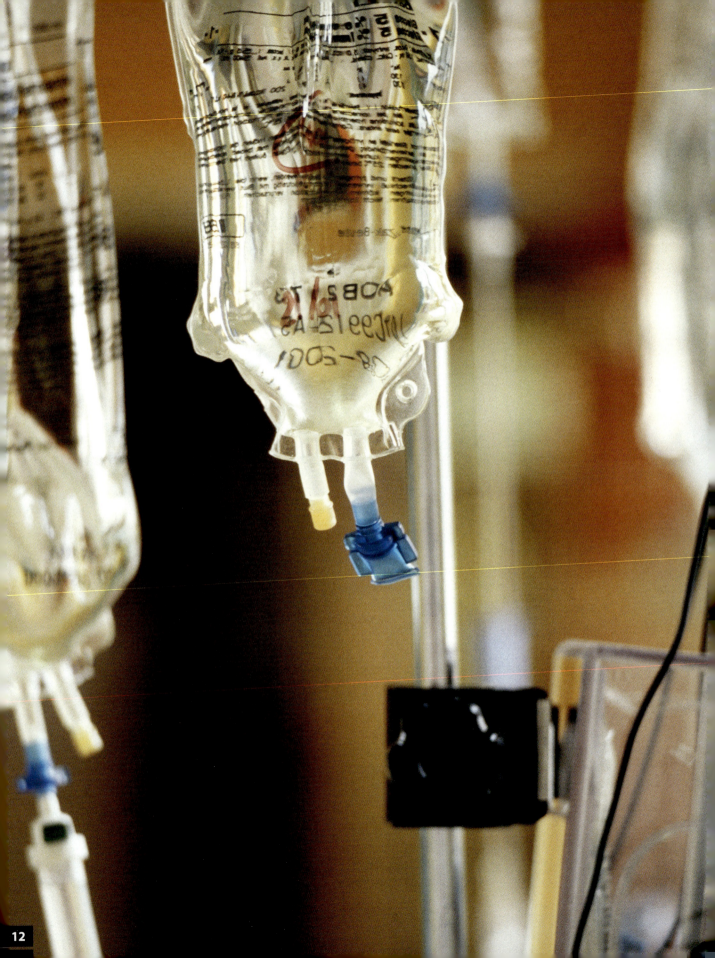

Medicinal Drugs

Humans have always used medicinal drugs. Early peoples learned the medical value of different plants by trial and error. Over time, many traditional remedies have been lost. Of those that have survived, some have been adopted by pharmaceutical companies. A well-known example is aspirin, the discovery of which is linked to the folk remedy of chewing willow bark to cure fever and headaches. Bayer introduced aspirin in 1899, and it has gone on to become the best-selling drug ever.

Opium, coca, and cannabis have arguably had more medical influence throughout history than any other plants. Paregoric, which is opium with a chemical antiseptic called camphor, and laudanum are traditional remedies for diarrhea and stomachache. Since the 1880s, cocaine has been used as a local anesthetic. Local anesthetics eliminate the need to render patients unconscious during some surgeries.

By-products of the opium poppy include codeine, the world's most popular cough suppressant, the painkiller morphine, and heroin. Bayer introduced heroin in the 1890s as a safer and quicker-acting version of morphine. Heroin was eventually outlawed for medical use. Although classified as having high abuse potential, codeine, morphine, and cocaine could be used under strict medical supervision. Cocaine

> *Most opiate abuse is from prescription drug derivatives, not from illegal heroin or opium.*

is still used today—although rarely—as a local anesthetic.

Some psychoactive drugs, such as opiates, stimulants, depressants, or hallucinogens, may be useful for medical treatment, but they easily can be abused if not taken under supervision. Most opiate abuse is from prescription drug derivatives, not from illegal heroin or opium. Codeine, along with meperidine (Demerol) and oxycodone (OxyContin) are commonly-abused painkillers.

In the 1950s, barbiturates, popular as sleeping pills, caused many accidental deaths. The development of **benzodiazepines** such as diazepam (Valium) and temazepam (Restoril) introduced a safer type of calming pill. These types of products have been widely used as anti-anxiety drugs even though they can lead to addiction and even death if combined with other drugs including alcohol. Valium-dependence can be especially dangerous in the elderly for whom it may exacerbate mental confusion and memory loss. A strong benzodiazepine known as Rohypnol has become a notorious club drug associated with cases of date rape.

Prescription drug spending in the United States was 11 percent of total health care spending in 2003, doubling as a share of expenditures over the past decade. The average cost of prescription drugs in the United States in 2004 was $95.86.

Most pharmaceutical drugs are sold as over-the-counter products. A few thousand can be dispensed only via a doctor's prescription. Despite this constraint, more than 3 billion prescriptions are issued in the United States each year, and global prescription sales crossed the $500 billion threshold in 2004.

An intravenous (IV) drip unit infuses fluids into a vein. An IV provides easy access to the bloodstream for drugs.

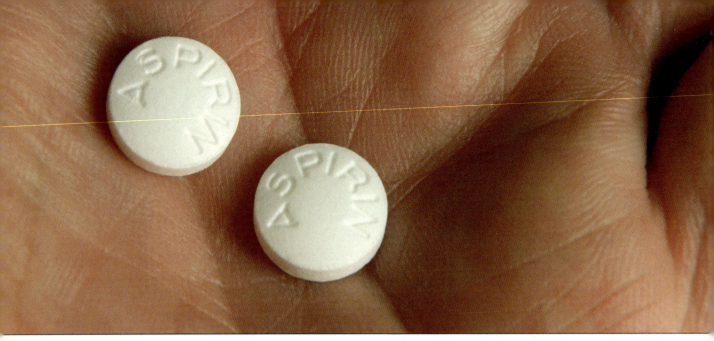

▬ Aspirin can be used to reduce fevers, swelling, and, in some cases, pain. They inhibit the production of prostaglandins, which are bodily chemicals responsible for sensitizing nerve endings to pain.

Huge amounts of money are being spent on drugs to alleviate depression and stress. Antidepressants are the best-selling drugs in America, with 2005 sales totalling $16 billion. Antidepressants are the best-selling drugs in the United States, with 2001 sales totalling $12.5 billion. Anti-ulcer drugs are the second-best sellers. As with many other drugs, concerns have been raised about the health impact of long-term anti-depressant use. Other fast-growing categories are drugs to aid sexual function, reduce obesity, fight nicotine addiction, and combat Alzheimer's disease.

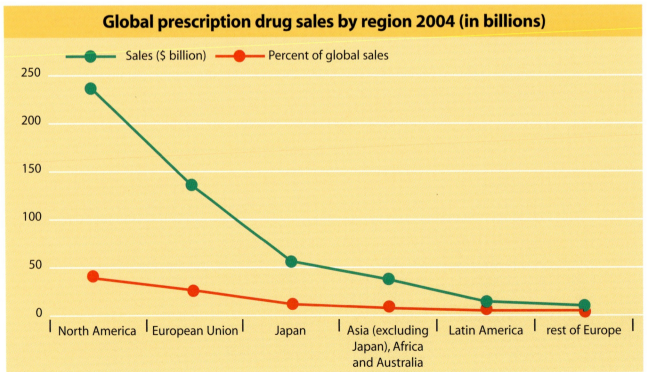

Source: Pharmaceutical Executive, May 2005

Understanding Global Issues—Substance Use And Abuse

DEBATING THE MEDICAL USE OF MARIJUANA

Extracts of hemp were used as remedies for numerous ailments in China, India, and medieval Europe. A century ago, cannabis products were widely marketed in the United States. Although U.S. law effectively banned the medical use of marijuana in 1937, 12 states have allowed marijuana to be used for medical purposes. Tincture of cannabis, a mixture of alcohol and cannabis, was a legal medicine in Great Britain until 1973. Canada first banned marijuana in 1923, but in July 2001, adopted a system regulating medical use of marijuana. Although medical use of marijuana is permitted, possession of marijuana for recreational use remains illegal in Canada. Some speculate that cannabis will soon be reintroduced throughout the world as a legal health remedy. There are a number of arguments for and against legalizing this drug.

PROS

Chemotherapy, as well as providing relief for sufferers of arthritis and multiple sclerosis. It has also been used to successfully treat people suffering from depression. These health benefits outweigh the risks.

Long-term side effects and addiction are irrelevant in treating seriously or terminally ill patients.

Studies have shown that cannabinoids, marijuana-like drugs, suppress pain.

Smoking marijuana carries no risk of death.

Marijuana can be used as a blood thinner, preventing the formation of blood clots.

Marijuana has been shown to lower bad cholesterol by up to 35 percent in 60 days.

CONS

Smoking marijuana affects the brain, leading to impaired short-term memory, perception, judgment, and motor skills.

Smoking three joints, or marijuana cigarettes, has the same effect on the lungs as smoking 20 cigarettes. Respiratory problems can develop, such as chronic bronchitis and inflamed sinuses. Smoking marijuana may also promote cancer of the respiratory tract and lungs.

Long-term marijuana use can lead to addiction for some people. Many people experience difficulty when they try to stop using the drug because of craving and withdrawal symptoms.

Frequent, heavy marijuana users can develop tolerance for the drug, meaning that they require increasingly larger doses of the drug to get the same desired results as obtained from previously smaller amounts.

▎ In 2005, Afghanistan produced a "record opium poppy harvest," according to the International Narcotics Control Board.

DRUGS AND HEALTH

Many drugs that improve physiological conditions are also psychoactive drugs that affect the brain. Drugs can stabilize the imbalances in neurotransmitter distribution experienced by people with afflictions such as bipolar disorder. The heavy concentration and unregulated movement of drugs in and out of synapses can also have negative impacts—within the immediate brain region and in other parts of the body. For example, morphine reduces pain and enhances euphoria in addicts, but it also reduces the brain's production of opiates, and so extends the addiction.

Ritalin, a mild stimulant and chemical relative of amphetamines, is widely used to remedy attention deficit hyperactivity disorder (ADHD) in children. By the late 1990s, several million U.S. children were being prescribed Ritalin.

KEY CONCEPTS

Depressants Depressants are a class of drugs that slow the rate of the body's vital functions. Alcohol and sleeping pills are commonly-used depressants.

Hallucinogens Substances, especially drugs, that distort perception and conjure fantastic images in users are called hallucinogens. LSD is one well-known hallucinogen.

Opiates Drugs that contain opium or an opium derivative, such as morphine or heroin, are called opiates. Opiates are compounds extracted from the opium poppy and their chemical derivatives. These drugs have a relaxing, pacifying, or dulling effect, and may cause sleepiness.

Stimulants Drugs or other agents that produce a temporary increase in the functional activity of a body part or organ are called stimulants. Caffeine is a common stimulant found in coffee, tea, and soft drinks.

Understanding Global Issues—Substance Use And Abuse

Pharmacist

Position: Pharmacist
Duties: Prepares and dispenses drugs prescribed by physicians and other health practitioners, and counsels patients on drug side effects and interactions
Education: Doctor of Pharmacy (Pharm.D.), must also pass the licensure examination of a state board of pharmacy
Interests: Chemistry, biology, medicine, helping others

For more information on a career as a pharmacist, visit the American Association of Colleges of Pharmacy at **www.aacp.org**, or visit **www.nacds.org** for the National Association of Chain Drug Stores.

Careers in Focus

Pharmacy is a branch of medical science that deals with the sources, nature, properties, and preparation of drugs. Pharmacists are specially trained to dispense drugs and provide drug-related information to patients. Pharmacists may practice in a pharmacy located in a hospital, nursing home, or in a community-based pharmacy. They may work for managed care organizations or consulting firms. Pharmaceutical companies also hire pharmacists to conduct scientific research or to aid in the development and production of new pharmaceutical products.

Compounding, the mixing of ingredients to form powders, tablets, capsules, and ointments, is only a small part of a pharmacist's duties. Pharmaceutical companies produce many drugs in standard doses so that pharmacists do not need to compound them. Often, pharmacists are called on to make decisions about drug therapy and patient counseling. Pharmacists counsel patients about adverse reactions or interactions of prescription drugs. They also provide information about over-the-counter drugs and make recommendations to patients about what drugs are suitable for them. Pharmacists who work in hospitals assess, plan, and monitor drug programs for people staying in the hospital.

Pharmacists must have strong decision-making, listening, and organizational skills. Pharmacists may operate a pharmacy, performing tasks that include ordering drugs and maintaining records, as well as managing the staff.

Accepted Social Drugs

Most people do not think of a cup of tea as a drug. A large cup of strong black tea may contain 100 milligrams of caffeine—about the same amount as one cup of coffee or two cans of cola. Caffeine stimulates heart rate and brain activity. Combined with sugar, caffeine can produce an energy surge. Excessive amounts of sugar can alter behavior, making people hyperactive or aggressive. In other words, even food can be psychoactive.

Medically, caffeine can be used as a heart stimulant and as a mild diuretic, as it increases urine production. Recreationally,

It takes 15 to 35 hours for 95 percent of caffeine to be eliminated from the body.

caffeine provides a boost of energy or feelings of heightened alertness. People use caffeine to stay awake for longer periods of time, especially college students and drivers. Many people feel they cannot function in the morning without the caffeine a cup of coffee provides to give them a boost.

Caffeine is an addictive drug. It stimulates the brain in the same ways as amphetamines, cocaine, and heroin, although to a lesser degree. Once caffeine's effects wear off, users face fatigue and depression. Caffeine has tremendous impact on sleep. Half of caffeine is absorbed by

BINGE DRINKING AND ALCOPOPS

In Great Britain and North America, drinking among youths aged 12–17 has grown rapidly in recent years. Though all 50 U.S. states have banned alcohol sales to anyone under 21, there has been relatively little impact on teenage drinking habits. More than 70 percent of American students drink alcohol, and half drink heavily at least once per month. Binge drinking is part of student culture on many campuses in both Great Britain and the United States. It is not as prevalent in continental Europe, where children tend to be introduced to alcohol gradually and from an early age.

The marketing of alcopops—soft drinks that contain alcohol—is a recent development that has probably contributed to adolescent drinking. Previous generations of youth were deterred by the bitter taste of traditional beer, wine, and spirits, but youths accustomed to sweet soft drinks slip easily into drinking alcopops. Companies in businesses as diverse as fast food and banking have realized that youths provide an excellent target for building brand awareness and lifetime buying habits. However, consumer groups question the ethics of such strategies.

▮▮▮ World beer consumption has fallen by 20 percent over the past 25 years.

Understanding Global Issues—Substance Use And Abuse

the body in about 6 hours. It takes about 15 to 35 hours, however, for 95 percent of caffeine to be eliminated from the body. Although a person who consumes caffeine may be able to fall asleep, the body often misses out on the benefits of deep sleep.

Caffeine has been suggested as a possible cause of cancer and birth defects, but no studies have confirmed these findings. The United States Food and Drug Administration (FDA) does not include caffeine on its list of "generally recognized as safe" (GRAS) drugs, but acknowledges no clear evidence of hazard at normal levels of use.

Despite the possible health risks of ingesting caffeine, soft drink consumption has increased steadily in the **developed world** over the last 50 years. In the United States, the average consumption of soft drinks is 56 gallons (212 liters) per person per year. Many children habitually drink several colas a day. Caffeine consumption varies greatly by country. Per capita consumption in the United States is 211 mg per day. In Sweden, it is 425 mg per day, and in Great Britain, it is 444 mg per day. Some argue that aggressive marketing is ultimately to blame for increased consumption of products that can cause long-term health damage. A more obvious target for this claim is the tobacco industry.

Tobacco is the most damaging drug used in human society. Nicotine is highly toxic and highly addictive. Cigarettes kill half of all lifetime users, about 4.2 million people worldwide, an impact disguised by the slow pace of its health effects. In 1998, the tobacco

> *Cigarettes kill half of all lifetime users, about 4.2 million people worldwide.*

industry agreed to pay the 50 U.S. states about $250 billion over 25 years to compensate them for the costs of treating tobacco-related illnesses.

Although it is an accepted medical fact that tobacco smoking causes cancer and other potentially fatal illnesses, youth smoking has increased in recent years and runs at about one quarter of the adult population. Most adult smokers took up the habit during their teenage years. Average per capita consumption in the United States is four cigarettes per day. About 80 percent of regular smokers are addicted to nicotine, whereas only 34 percent of heroin users and 21 percent of cocaine users are addicted.

The World Health Organization (WHO) has campaigned strongly for tougher controls on tobacco sales. WHO is especially concerned about advertisements in the **developing world** that claim smoking is sexy or enhances manhood.

QUITTING CALENDAR
THE BENEFITS OF STOPPING SMOKING

1 day later	Heart, blood pressure, and blood show improvements
1 year later	Excess risk of coronary heart disease is half that of a continuing smoker
5–15 years later	Risk of a stroke is reduced to that of never-smokers
10 years later	Risk of lung cancer is reduced to less than half that of continuing smokers; risk of many other cancers decrease
15 years later	Risk of coronary heart disease is similar to that of never-smokers, and the overall risk of death almost the same, especially if the smoker quits before illness develops

Source: World Health Organization

WHO predicts that smoking-related deaths—currently 4 million per year worldwide—will rise to 10 million per year by 2030. The World Bank estimates that as many as 500 million people alive today will eventually die of tobacco-related diseases.

In the United States, the FDA regards cigarettes as drug delivery devices and asserts its right to place restrictions on cigarette advertising and vending. The big international tobacco companies have seen sales dwindle in North America as a non-smoking culture has gradually taken hold.

Evidence that passive smoking or second-hand smoke is almost as bad as direct inhalation has led to a ban on smoking in most public places in the United States. In contrast, visitors to southern or eastern Europe quickly notice that most people, young and old, smoke cigarettes. As sales have dwindled in North America, tobacco sales in the developing world have grown strongly. There is huge scope for further expansion, bearing in mind the gap between smoking prevalence rates for men and women. In China, 60 percent of adults are smokers, but only 7 percent of women smoke. In India, 40 percent of men and 3 percent of women smoke.

In many parts of the world, tobacco use often accompanies alcohol use. Alcohol is also a widely used social drug that is not harmful to health if used in moderation. Those who drink in moderation live longer on

---

In 19th century America, alcohol consumption was very high—about five times higher per person than it is today.

---

average than those who do not drink at all. Unfortunately, many people do not drink moderately.

Alcohol has always presented governments with control difficulties. Such problems were exacerbated by the wide availability of distilled spirits in crowded urban areas after the Industrial Revolution. In 19th-century America, alcohol consumption was very high—about five times higher per person than it is today. By the 1820s, people were drinking an average 7 gallons (27 l) of pure alcohol per person per year. Statistics show that Prohibition reduced the annual per capita consumption from 2.6 gallons (9.8 l) during 1906–1910 to 0.97 gallons (3.7 l) after Prohibition ended in 1934.

One way to deter smoking and alcohol abuse is to make cigarettes and alcohol prohibitively expensive. This route, however, likely will lead to black markets, and illegal suppliers will emerge to meet heavy customer demand. Most societies, therefore, tolerate a certain level of indulgence in habits that are known to be harmful. They do this by controlling the strength of substances, regulating their supply, and taxing them at bearable levels.

■ By 2006, Washington and Georgia had joined 11 other states to prohibit smoking in most public places.

Understanding Global Issues—Substance Use And Abuse

Estimates suggest worldwide deaths related to smoking will reach 10 million a year by 2020.

KEY CONCEPTS

Passive smoking Exposure to the smoke exhaled by tobacco smokers and the smoke given off by the burning end of cigarettes—called environmental tobacco smoke (ETS) or second-hand smoke—is referred to as passive smoking. ETS is responsible for about 3,000 lung cancer deaths in nonsmoking adults each year and impairs the respiratory health of hundreds of thousands of children.

U.S. Food and Drug Administration (FDA) The FDA is a department of the United States Department of Health and Human Services. This department administers food, drug, cosmetic, and related laws. The FDA ensures foods are pure and wholesome and are produced under sanitary conditions. It ensures the safety of drugs and therapeutic devices. The FDA ensures cosmetics are safe and made from appropriate ingredients and that labels and packaging are accurate.

World Health Organization (WHO) Established in 1948, WHO is the United Nations agency for health. The goal of WHO is to achieve the highest possible level of health for everyone. For WHO, health is not just about the absence of disease. Health includes complete physical, mental, and social well being. WHO works with governments and nongovernmental organizations to promote and carry out effective health policies.

Accepted Social Drugs

Illicit Social Drugs

While cannabis, cocaine, and opiates dominate the black market, a number of other substances, many of them synthetic, have appeared on the drug scene. Many drugs are synthetically produced in illegal laboratories. Street drugs are often faked or **adulterated**.

Cannabis is by far the most commonly used illicit drug. It is produced from the hemp plant. The leaves and flowering tops of the cannabis plant are smoked as marijuana. The main intoxicating effect of marijuana comes from delta-9-tetrahydro-cannabinol (THC). In the 1960s, marijuana had a typical THC content of less than one percent. Today, it may be 5–10 times as strong.

According to the UN, there are more than 140 million cannabis abusers worldwide. More than one third of the population in the United States and Great Britain over the age of 12 have smoked marijuana at some time in their life.

Smoking a marijuana joint produces a mild euphoria—a feeling referred to as a "high"—lasting several hours, as well as some loss of concentration and memory ability. Regular marijuana users have a reputation for lack of energy

■ **Marijuana is not known to cause a physical dependence or extreme discomfort from withdrawal. However, frequent users have been known to become psychologically accustomed to the drug.**

and motivation, but a causal effect has not yet been proven. At present, there is no convincing evidence of significant health damage, but it is too soon to know how the stronger cannabis products of recent years will affect long-term users. A further complication is that normal-strength marijuana is often combined with other drugs, which are often more harmful. Mixing drugs, or polyuse, is common, but it greatly increases the health risks to the user.

Cannabis is smoked in many different parts of the world, even where it is officially banned. There are other ways to ingest cannabis besides smoking. In India, for example, a liquid form of cannabis known as *bhang* is also popular.

In the United States, cannabis is often taken as seedless buds known as sinsemilla with a typical THC content of 10–15 percent. **Resin** scraped off the plant is known as hashish and has a typical THC content of 10–20 percent.

Cocaine, derived from the coca plant, is another popular illicit drug. The average purity of street cocaine is about 60 percent. Most cocaine is snorted up one nostril, resulting in a powerful sensation of pleasure and energy (the high), often followed by feelings of deep depression. Cocaine increases heart rate, elevates blood pressure, and dilates the pupils. A typical cocaine high lasts for about an hour. Cocaine can also be dissolved in water and injected. The high temperature of smoking cocaine destroys the psychoactive ingredients. A purified form of cocaine known as freebase can be smoked through a **water pipe**, giving an almost instant high. The danger with freebase comes from lingering fumes that can cause explosions. Freebase is obtained by purifying cocaine in a solution. Smoked or injected cocaine produces a faster and shorter-lasting high.

It is too soon to know how the stronger cannabis products of recent years will affect long-term users.

Crack is the street name for another form of smokable cocaine that is safer than freebase. Crack is a concentrated form of cocaine that has been shaped into pellets or broken into small pieces and placed in a special smoking apparatus. When heated, the rocks crackle, hence the term "crack."

Crack was introduced in the 1980s. It quickly became popular because it was cheaper to buy and faster than cocaine in its delivery to the brain. In the United States, the devastating popularity of crack caused Ronald Reagan's government to intensify its efforts in the war on drugs.

Regular cocaine use can lead to addiction, depression, nervous irritability, and paranoia. Chronic cocaine use can also lead to skin abscesses, nose septum perforations, weight loss, and damage to the nervous system. Negative psychological effects, including extreme restlessness, anxiety, irritability, and even paranoid psychosis, can occur. Even a small dose of cocaine can cause death, usually from seizures or heart attacks. In the United States, cocaine is classified as a narcotic. It causes strong psychological dependence.

While cocaine is a powerful stimulant, opium and its derivatives produce a dreamlike or dissociative euphoria that banishes physical pain and emotional concerns. The opium poppy is the source of a range of drugs, of which heroin is regarded as the most habit-forming.

Heroin is processed from morphine, a naturally-occurring substance extracted from the seedpod of the Asian poppy plant. Asian heroin is usually a white powder, while Latin American heroin is often brown. The price of heroin fluctuates, but the general trend has been a price decrease.

Traditionally, heroin has been injected. Injection is the most efficient way to administer low-purity heroin and achieve a high. In addition to initial feelings of euphoria, short-term effects of heroin include a warm flushing of the skin, dry mouth, and heavy extremities.

After the initial euphoria, heroin users experience an alternately wakeful and drowsy state, often feeling drowsy for several hours. As the central nervous system depresses, mental functioning becomes clouded. Breathing can slow down to the point that respiratory failure occurs.

Most buyers have no way of knowing what has been added to heroin powder. Before sale, heroin powder is often adulterated with other substances.

Uncertainty over the strength and quality of the product is a significant cause of deaths from

> *Some amphetamine users experience formication, the belief that the flesh is crawling with insects.*

heroin overdoses. Purity of heroin rose sharply in the mid-1990s. Before that time, nearly all heroin sold in America was so heavily diluted it was rarely more than 10 percent pure. By the mid 1990s, however, purity was routinely at 50–60 percent.

The availability of high-purity heroin and the fear of contracting diseases, such as Acquired Immune Deficiency Syndrome (AIDS) or hepatitis, from sharing needles has made snorting and smoking the drug more common. Some users also mistakenly believe that, unlike injection, snorting or smoking the drug will not lead to addiction. Heroin addicts typically need two injections each day to avoid unpleasant withdrawal symptoms.

Amphetamines are another class of commonly used drugs. These drugs are chemically similar to adrenaline and produce intense feelings of power and alertness. These stimulant drugs induce exhilarating feelings of power, strength, focus, and enhanced motivation. The need for sleep and food is diminished. The euphoria may last for several hours, but it is followed by intense mental depression and fatigue. When taken in high doses or used long term, amphetamines can cause difficulty breathing, dizziness, faintness, increased blood pressure, mood or mental changes, a pounding heartbeat, and unusual tiredness or

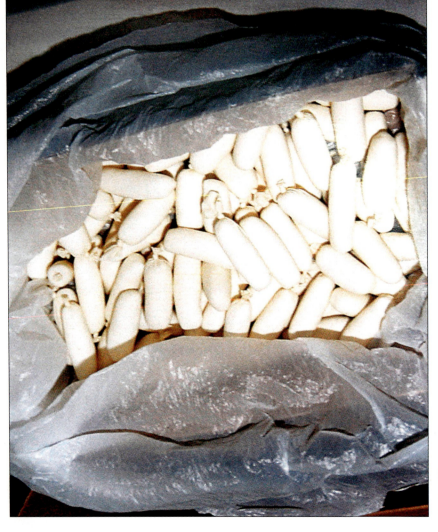

■ **In 2004, 3.1 million Americans aged 12 and older reported having tried heroin in the past.**

weakness. Some amphetamine users experience formication, the belief that their flesh is crawling with insects.

During World War II, soldiers and politicians used amphetamines as valuable concentration aids during long

> **Marketed as Ecstasy, the drug quickly found its way onto the club scene.**

periods of emergency. Winston Churchill, prime minister of Great Britain during World War II, regularly used Benzedrine to stay alert and relied on barbiturates to help him sleep. Adolf Hitler preferred to use the fast-acting drug methamphetamine. Some people today use amphetamines to stay awake or increase productivity. Such effects are short-lived.

Hallucinogenic drugs are mild stimulants that affect neurotransmitters in the brain, causing extraordinary visions and changes in perception. The sensations are often either very pleasant or extremely disturbing. Hallucinogens cause the pupils to dilate, some arteries to constrict, blood pressure to rise, and certain spinal reflexes to become increasingly excitable.

LSD is the best-known and most potent hallucinogen. LSD is often added to absorbent paper and divided into small decorated squares. A mere 25 micrograms of LSD produce a psychedelic impact. During the 1960s and early 1970s, the dosage ranged from 100–200 micrograms. Today, a dosage of LSD is more likely to range from 20–80 micrograms. In addition to short-term effects on perception and mood, LSD is associated with psychotic-like episodes that can occur long after a person has taken the drug. An LSD experience is called a trip,

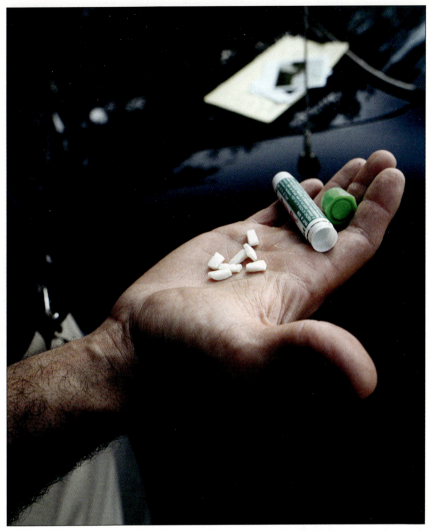

Cocaine was first used in 1855 as a local anesthetic in minor surgeries.

and it can last for 12 hours. In addition, many LSD users experience flashbacks. These include recurrences of certain aspects of the LSD experience without the user ever taking the drug again.

The hallucinogenic phencyclidine (PCP) was developed in the 1950s as an intravenous anesthetic. Its use in humans was discontinued in 1965 because users became agitated, delusional, and irrational.

Illicit Social Drugs **25**

■ Studies show that club drugs, such as Ecstasy, cause irreparable changes to the human brain. Brain damage and memory loss are common in frequent users of the drug.

PCP was introduced as a street drug in the 1960s. It quickly gained a reputation as a drug that could cause bad reactions and was not worth the risk.

Other well-known hallucinogens are mescaline, which occurs in the Peyote cactus, and psilocybin, which is also known as a magic mushroom. The effects of mescaline last about 12 hours, while psilocybin effects last for only 4–7 hours.

Psychologists in the 1970s used MDMA to enhance empathy and social communication. Marketed as Ecstasy, the drug quickly found its way onto the club scene. MDMA gives temporary feelings of euphoria at the same time that it interferes with **serotonin receptors** in the brain. It seems likely that MDMA use will cause long-term damage in regular users, but this research has not been completed.

KEY CONCEPTS

Acquired Immune Deficiency Syndrome (AIDS) AIDS is a disease of the immune system that is caused by infection with the human immunodeficiency virus (HIV). HIV destroys certain white blood cells and is transmitted through blood or bodily secretions. AIDS patients lose the ability to fight infections, often dying from secondary causes, such as pneumonia. AIDS can be spread through sharing needles.

Narcotics The term narcotic primarily applies to opiates. Opoids, synthesized chemical compounds that resemble opiates in their effects, are also narcotics. Narcotics lessen pain, not only by decreasing the perception of pain, but also by altering the reaction to it.

Biography
Karen Tandy

Born: October 24, 1953, in Tarrant County, Texas
Education: Bachelor's degree in Science in Education, law degree from the Texas School of Law
Legacy: Appointed Administrator of the Drug Enforcement Agency (DEA) on July 31, 2003

Visit **www.usdoj.gov/dea/ agency/administrator.htm** for more information about Tandy and other DEA officials. Also click on **www.whitehousedrug policy.gov** to learn about drug policy in the United States.

People in Focus

Prior to becoming DEA Administrator, Karen Tandy was associate deputy attorney general and director of the Organized Crime Drug Enforcement Task Forces (OCDETF). As such, she was responsible for the day-to-day management of the Drug Enforcement Administration and the National Drug Intelligence Center, as well as for developing national drug enforcement policy and strategies. Tandy worked in several key positions in the Criminal Division of the Department of Justice between 1990 and 1999, supervising the department's drug and forfeiture litigation. As deputy chief of the Narcotics and Dangerous Drug Section, she supervised the department's narcotic prosecutions nationwide. As the first deputy chief at the Special Operations Division, she managed the implementation of the nationwide coordination of drug wiretap investigations.

Between 1979 and 1990, Tandy was an assistant United States attorney. She prosecuted many highly complicated cases involving violent crimes, drugs, money laundering, and forfeiture. Before joining the Justice Department, she was a clerk to the chief judge of the Northern District of Texas. Tandy has received the Attorney General's Award for Distinguished Service, the Department of Justice Award for Extraordinary Achievement, and the United States Attorney Director's Award for Superior Service. Tandy was born in Fort Worth, Texas. She and holds degrees from Texas Tech University and Texas Tech Law School.

Mapping Problem Drugs

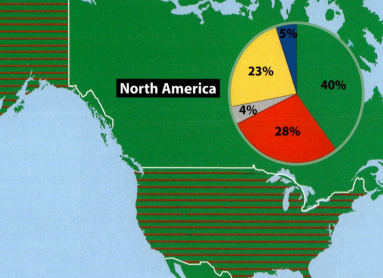

Figure 1: Worldwide Problem Drugs
As of 2003, the main problem drugs, as outlined by the United Nations Office on Drugs and Crime (UNODC), were opiates and cocaine. Based on treatment demand, these drugs continue to lead in most nations; however, in East and South-East Asia, the main problem drugs are amphetamine-type stimulants (ATS). Cannibis is the main problem drug with reference to treatment demand in Africa.

- Opiates
- Cannabis
- Cocaine-type
- Amphetamine-type stimulants
- Others
- No information available

Source: UNODC, Annual Reports Questionnaire Data/DELTA and National Government Reports

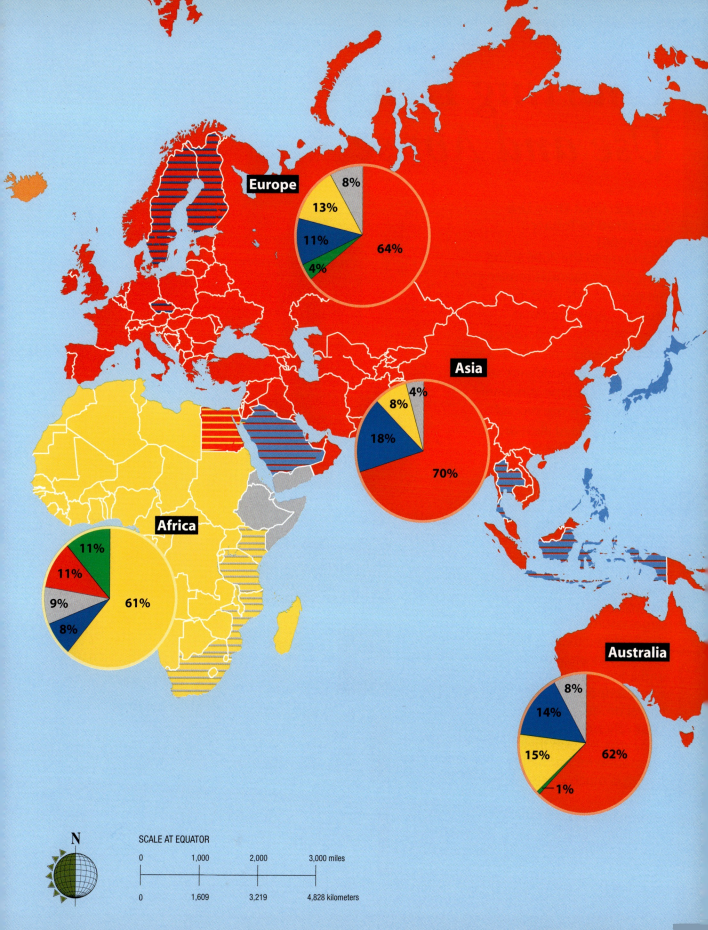

Mapping Problem Drugs

Charting Drug Use and Abuse

Figure 2: Illicit Drug Use Compared to Tobacco Use (2006)
According to the 2006 *World Drug Report*, cannibis remains the most widely used illicit drug. It is estimated that about 162 million people use cannibis worldwide. About 35 million people worldwide use amphetamine-type stimulants (ATS), making it the second most widely used illicit drug. However, 1.7 billion people worldwide use tobacco.

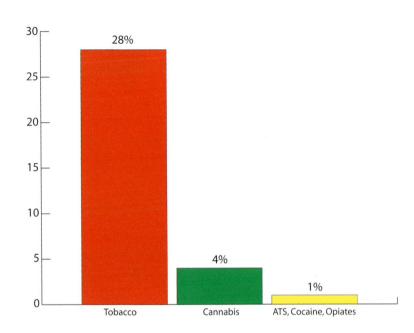

Figure 3: Drug-related Deaths in the United States
Tobacco causes the largest number of drug-related deaths, followed by alcohol and adverse reactions to prescription drugs. Illegal drugs cause a relatively small number of deaths, though their reputation for harming health is much worse.

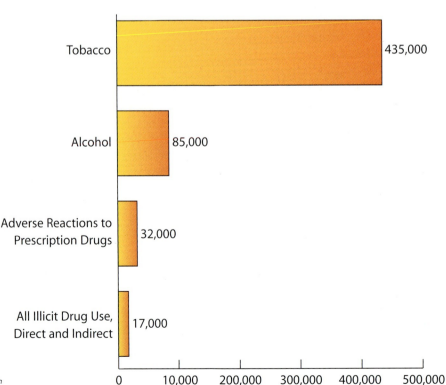

Source: Journal of the American Medical Association

Figure 4: Drug Use in Schools
The University of Michigan carries out an annual survey of drug use among American students. The figures from the 2005 survey show trends in the lifetime prevalence of drug use. The European Monitoring Centre for Drugs and Drug Addiction records the same information for the European Union.

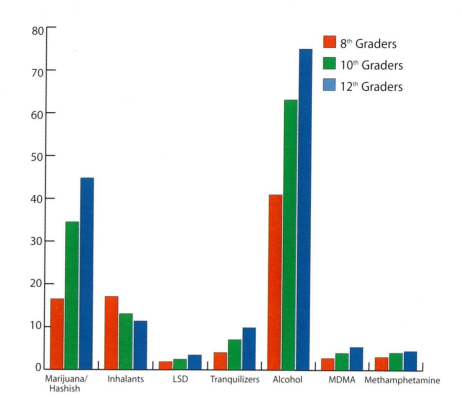

Figure 5: Number of Cannabis Users Worldwide
According to the National Survey on Drug Use and Health (NSDUH), about 25 million people over the age of 12 used cannibis in 2003. Of them, 14.5 million said they had used the drug in the past month. This is very similar to surveys conducted in other parts of the world.

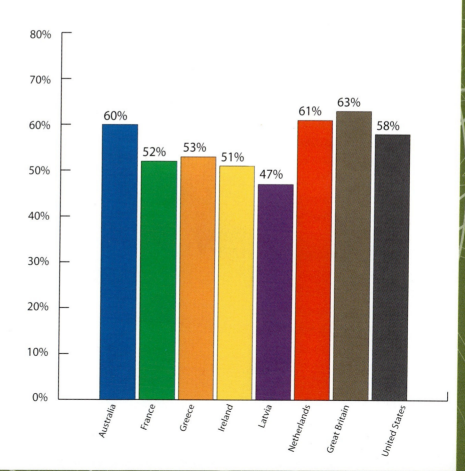

Charting Drug Use and Abuse 31

Drugs and Crime

Attempts to limit the availability of drugs that are in high demand has spawned the development of powerful global crime networks. No one can be sure how much money organized crime makes from producing and trafficking illegal drugs, but the sums are undoubtedly huge. High sales are generated without advertising. The UN estimates that global turnover in illicit drugs is worth about $400 billion per year.

Criminals have always thrived when official markets have been unable to provide the goods that people want. The money made from black market opium in 19th-century China helped to develop the power of the triad gangs and their overseas networks. Prohibition in 1920's America boosted organized crime. **Bootleggers** took control of all trade in beer, wine, and spirits. Some of the gangs shifted into the narcotics market when Prohibition ended.

The Cold War also arguably played a role in the spread of drug trafficking. Drug trafficking creates the most visible of organized crime profits, which have grown considerably since the Cold War ended.

The Vietnam conflict introduced thousands of American soldiers to cheap heroin. At the same time, the Central Intelligence Agency (CIA)

> *Criminals have always thrived when official markets have been unable to provide the goods that people want.*

was arranging deals with anti-communist drug barons in southeast and central Asia and in Latin America. Drug trafficking has often been used to finance **guerrilla** or terrorist operations.

Before 1979, Afghanistan's traditional opium crop was not a major factor in global drug trafficking and heroin production. After the Soviet invasion of Afghanistan and the resulting conflict from 1979–1982, American efforts to combat the spread of communism included CIA support for local warlords financed by drug trafficking. By the late 1990s, Afghanistan was the source of 70 percent of the world's heroin. In 2001, the Taliban banned opium farming. Production of gum, from which heroin is derived, dropped to 82 tons (74 t) in 2001 from 4,030 tons (3,656 t) in 2000. However, the war on terrorism saw the overthrow of the Taliban, and in 2005, Afghanistan's share of opium production was roughly 87 percent of the world total.

▬ During his bootlegging years, crime lord Al Capone estimated his annual profits to be about $60 million.

The government of Pakistan has made an effort to eliminate narcotics trafficking within its borders.

The illicit drug industry has developed dramatically over the years, adapting quickly to new trends and taking maximum advantage of opportunities presented by globalization. The industry has also taken advantage of new technology and money-laundering facilities.

Informal alliances between criminal groups are common and operate based on trust and threats of violence rather than legally enforceable contracts. Drugs are the ideal black market product. Heroin and cocaine—powders of very high value—are particularly attractive. These drugs are easy to smuggle, non-perishable, and far more profitable than whiskey. The profit margins for these drugs are huge. According to a UN report, what begins as freshly harvested opium in Central Asia at $41 per pound ($90 per kg) can become heroin sold on the streets of New York for $290,000. Coca leaves sold by a Colombian

> **Coca leaves sold for $600 may retail at $110,000 as cocaine powder.**

farmer for $600 may retail for $110,000 as cocaine powder.

Vast profits can also be made from club drugs, such as MDMA and other amphetamine-type stimulants. These drugs can be made for a few cents and sold for $10–20 per tablet. Until recently, production of MDMA was concentrated in the Netherlands. Israeli gangs have taken a major stake in the global trade of amphetamine-type stimulants. Most methamphetamines sold in the United States, however, are produced in Mexico.

Drug prices vary greatly depending on location, market trends, and the wealth of customers. Heroin, may be sold for as little as $10 a gram in Pakistan or as much as $2,000 a gram in New York. Plentiful supplies of drugs, though mainly destined for the rich markets of the West, have led to rapid increases in addiction in Asia in recent years. Pakistan is said to have well over a million addicts, Iran two million, and Russia at least three million, compared with about one million in the European Union.

Most illicit drugs are easy to adulterate, creating an obvious advantage for the criminal. Substitute drugs are sold to increase dealer profits. While the strengths of cocaine, heroin, and cannabis have increased over the past 20 years, club drugs are becoming increasingly adulterated. A pill sold as Ecstasy may contain no MDMA. Substitute drugs are sometimes sold in place of club drugs. For example, the MDMA-related drug paramethoxyamphetamine (PMA) has been used as a substitute for MDMA. As a result, users ingest more of the substance to attain a better high, which can result in an overdose death.

Drugs and Crime

Many drug dealers make a clear distinction between "dirty drugs," such as heroin and crack, and drugs such as amphetamines, cannabis, cocaine powder, and MDMA. These drugs are seen as relatively harmless recreational drugs, while heroin and crack are associated with addiction and crime. Heroin and other opiates have a pacifying effect, but crack and amphetamines can make people jumpy and prone to unpredictable and violent behavior. The need to feed an expensive habit can lead some addicts into petty crime, such as shoplifting, mugging, and car theft. According to some studies, nearly half of all robberies in Great Britain are attributable to illicit drugs.

Well-publicized destruction of seized drugs has more symbolic worth than practical effect. Based on UN figures, global seizures of opiates typically amount to about 15 percent of potential heroin production and about 40 percent of cocaine production, yet the seizure of 23 tons (21 t) of cocaine by the U.S. coast guard in 2000 barely affected the street price of cocaine.

> *According to some studies, nearly half of all robberies in Great Britain are attributable to illicit drugs.*

■ Statistics show that 25 percent of car thefts, 40 percent of robberies and assaults, and 50 percent of burglaries are committed by illicit drug users.

Understanding Global Issues—Substance Use And Abuse

In the Netherlands, cannabis can be purchased in "coffee shops."

DRUG POLICY IN THE NETHERLANDS

A common misperception is that the use of drugs is permitted throughout the Netherlands. Although drugs are not legalized, the laws are confusing and complicated.

The use of small quantities (5 g) of soft drugs, such as cannabis, is not a criminal offense. Use of smaller quantities (0.5 g) of hard drugs, such as cocaine and heroin, is generally tolerated. At the same time, all illicit drugs found during police searches of persons or places are systematically confiscated. The number of searches and seizures is rising dramatically. Importing, exporting, selling, trafficking, manufacturing, or growing illicit drugs is a crime subject to fines and/or imprisonment.

Although illegal according to the laws, "smoking coffee shops" in the Netherlands openly sell soft drugs. These coffee shops are permitted to keep drug supplies greater than the amounts permitted by law for personal use. However, they are only permitted to sell individual customers the amount legally permitted for personal use. In theory, the coffee shops cannot advertise drugs. They cannot sell alcohol on the same premises or allow clients to cause a public disturbance. These shops cannot sell drugs for takeout use or have more soft drugs on hand than the coffee shop conceivably needs to supply their clients' daily demands, an amount just over one pound (500 g).

In yet another paradox, wholesale suppliers to the smoking coffee shops remain criminals. Large-scale dealers are prosecuted to the full extent of the law, even if they do not supply users or coffee shops with more than the permitted amounts. How and where coffee shops obtain their supplies is, however, rarely investigated.

By law, cannabis remains a controlled substance in the Netherlands. Possession and production for personal use are offenses punishable by fines. However, a policy of nonenforcement has led to a situation where reliance upon nonenforcement has become common.

▬ The U.S. Drug Enforcement Administration's mission is to enforce the controlled substances laws and regulations.

It is virtually impossible to keep drugs out of a country. Drugs cannot even be kept out of prisons, where security measures are stringent. The drug problem in prisons shows how difficult it is to stop drugs from getting to those who want them. Decriminalization is advocated by some as a way to break the power of black markets and bootleggers, and to cut the need for addicts to resort to theft to get money for drugs.

KEY CONCEPTS

Cold War Journalist Walter Lippman first used the term "Cold War" to refer to the tensions that had developed between the United States and the former Soviet Union after the end of World War II. The Cold War resulted in two military alliances—the North Atlantic Treaty Organization (NATO), which represented the United States and its allies; and the Warsaw Pact, which represented the Soviet Union and its allies. While the United States and the Soviet Union never engaged in direct confrontation, many conflicts around the globe were linked to Cold War hostilities. The two countries did engage in an arms race, which saw a dramatic increase in the number of nuclear and other weapons produced in both countries. The Cold War ended around 1989, following the decline of Soviet power in Eastern Europe and the symbolic destruction of the Berlin Wall.

Triad gangs Triads are an intricate network of criminals that have roots in the 19th-century opium trade. The triads now operate in nearly every major center of the world. There are six main gangs, but more than 50 in total, that are essentially rivals at the local levels. However, they cooperate globally.

Federal Agent

Duties: Protect people's lives and property; enforce state and federal laws
Education: Bachelor's degree and some work experience in a related field
Interests: Justice, physical fitness, helping people

Visit **www.usdoj.gov/dea** for further information on qualifications and employment with the DEA. Also click on **www.atf.treas.gov** to learn about careers at the U.S. Bureau of Alcohol, Tobacco and Firearms.

Careers in Focus

Americans depend on police officers for protection. Police officers often work for different government agencies to specialize in an area of law enforcement. Two such agencies are the DEA and the Bureau of Alcohol, Tobacco and Firearms (ATF).

DEA agents enforce the federal laws and regulations that relate to illegal drugs. The DEA is the lead agency for domestic enforcement of these laws, and also has the sole responsibility for coordinating drug investigations outside of the U.S. agents conduct complex criminal investigations, carry out surveillance on criminals, and work undercover to bring illicit drug organizations to justice.

To become a special agent with the DEA, applicants must have a bachelor's degree, be a U.S. citizen between 21 and 36 years of age at time of appointment, be in excellent physical condition, successfully complete a background check to obtain top secret security clearance, and be willing to relocate to anywhere in the United States.

ATF special agents regulate and investigate violations of federal firearms and explosives laws and federal alcohol and tobacco regulations. ATF investigations involve surveillance, participation in raids, interviewing suspects and witnesses, making arrests, obtaining search warrants, and searching for physical evidence.

To be considered for the position of a special agent of the ATF, applicants must be a U.S. citizen between the ages of 21 and 37 at the time of appointment. Applicants must also successfully complete a field panel interview, pass a polygraph examination, complete a background investigation for top secret security clearance, pass a drug test, and passing a variety of examinations.

Careers in Focus

Controlling Drugs

Governments have a responsibility to control the availability of potentially harmful drugs, but there are widely differing views on how to best achieve this. Since 1990, U.S. policy has strongly influenced the attitude of Western governments to maintain drug control. This policy, which has focused on cutting off supply, originated in the moral attitudes that banned alcohol.

In 1900, cocaine was cheaper than alcohol. The Harrison Act of 1914 banned recreational use of opium and cocaine, restricting its use to medicinal products prescribed by doctors. Addicts were left with no choice but to turn to the black market for their drugs. The street price of heroin rose fifteenfold.

In 1917, Congress passed the Volstead Act, which prohibited the production and sale of alcohol. The act became effective in 1920, and its success has been widely argued. One argument proposes that rather than reduce overall alcohol consumption, the act changed Americans' drinking habits. Prohibition put far more emphasis on spirits, which were easier to smuggle than beer. Instead of generating revenue from taxes, prohibiting alcohol, cocaine, and opium transferred wealth to organized crime.

> *Addicts were left with no choice but to turn to the black market for their drugs.*

In 1930, Prohibition enforcer Harry J. Anslinger was put in charge of the Federal Bureau of Narcotics. He turned his attention to cannabis. At the time, hemp was widely grown in the United States for use in everything from clothing to paper. The recreational use of hemp as a pleasure-enhancing drug was also increasing.

The popularity of hemp among immigrants—unpopular during the Depression—gave Anslinger the chance to portray the "debauching" effects of cannabis. Anslinger remained head of the Federal Bureau of Narcotics until 1962, setting a fervent anti-drugs agenda.

■ **Police drug dogs are specially trained to sniff out drugs and alert authorities. Dogs are sometimes the only way to locate hidden narcotics.**

ESTIMATED DRUG USE AND ABUSE IN THE U.S.

Regular users of alcohol greatly exceed those for illicit drugs and include an estimated 12 million alcoholics. While the figures show only a small percentage of drinkers whose alcohol abuse requires medical treatment, this does not include long-term health damage such as cirrhosis of the liver and heart trouble.

Drug	Number of Users (millions)	Percent of Users Requiring Medical Treatment for Substance Abuse
Alcohol	138.5	0.3
Cannabis	19.5	1.0
Cocaine	4.2	5.3
Amphetamines	1.7	4.0
Crack Cocaine	1.4	11.9
Heroin	1.0	20.0
Methamphetamine	0.8	6.6

Drug-taking became associated with "unAmerican activities," weakening society and corrupting the young. However, the 1960s brought a new wave of drug experimentation to America. The Comprehensive Drug Abuse Prevention and Control Act of 1970 became the foundation of renewed U.S. efforts to regulate narcotics and other mind-altering substances that were in circulation.

In 1971, President Nixon declared a "war on drugs" and moved regulatory control from the FDA to the newly-formed Drug Enforcement Administration (DEA), a branch of the Department of Justice. The DEA received money and extra enforcement powers. As drug abuse continued and crack cocaine appeared on the streets, President Reagan introduced mandatory minimum sentences for drug offenses. The prison population rose sharply as judges sentenced those in possession of even small amounts of drugs for periods of 5 to 40 years.

By the mid-1990s, drug offenders made up nearly one quarter of the prison population. Federal and state anti-drug spending rose tenfold during the 1990s to a total of almost $40 billion a year.

Demand for drugs did not lessen, and the street price of the most popular illegal substances halved during this period—clear proof that the attempt to limit the supply was not working.

Even so, Congress gave approval to projects such as Operation Libertador and Plan Colombia, supporting military efforts to destroy coca fields throughout the Andes. In 2001, more than 309 square miles (80,000 ha) of coca fields in Colombia were sprayed with herbicide. Environmental damage was added to the list of evils associated with the war on drugs.

By the late 1990s, informed opinion on both sides of the Atlantic Ocean was pressing for a change in the policy approach to drugs.

▬▬ **In 1971, U.S. President Richard Nixon called illicit substances "America's public enemy number one."**

Understanding Global Issues—Substance Use And Abuse

▬ Cocaine destined for Europe and the United States often passes through northern Arica, Chile. In 2000, Chilean authorities seized and destroyed 9 tons (8 t) of cocaine from one shipment in Arica.

THE IMPACT OF LEGALIZATION

A study published in 1999 by the Western Economic Association International concluded that marijuana decriminalization in the United States would increase the probability of marijuana use by about 8 percent, while decriminalization of cocaine and heroin might lead to about 260,000 new regular cocaine users and 47,000 new regular heroin users. Most experts agree that legalization would increase the number of users, though views differ strongly on the long-term impact. Societies normally adjust to new drugs, settling into a pattern where there is a small proportion of addicts, a substantial number of occasional users or experimenters, and a majority of abstainers.

Key benefits of legalization include tax revenues that could be generated from duties on psychotropic substances, as well as damaging organized crime through the collapse of black markets that sell presently illegal drugs.

Governments that want to legalize drugs would first have to step out of the constraints imposed by the 1961 UN Convention on Drugs, which addressed trafficking and abuse of natural or synthetic narcotics, cannabis and cocaine. The 1971 convention added hallucinogens, amphetamines, barbiturates, sedatives, and tranquilizers, and the 1988 convention included illicit traffic. It would be difficult for a single state to opt for legalization against U.S. and UN opposition. There is also the risk of becoming a haven for drugs. The Netherlands has a relatively low rate of marijuana users among its own population, but it has attracted plenty of visitors from abroad.

Controlling Drugs

Many argued that the war on drugs had been massively counter-productive and that the focus of attention should be moved from prevention to harm reduction.

Some U.S. states had voted for policy reforms such as legalizing medical marijuana. Others were paying more attention to drug treatment, needle exchange, and, above all, education. "Just say know," it was argued, was likely to be more effective than "Just say no." In this respect independent organizations, such as Dance Safe, which provides factual information about drugs and the risks they carry, have more credibility with the young than government advertising campaigns.

More than 70 percent of the money spent annually by the United States on drug control is used for cutting supply and for catching and punishing drug dealers, not on reducing demand or treating drug abusers. In Europe, the trend is toward shifting the emphasis of drug policy from punishment to education and treatment. Great Britain, for example, allocated 62 percent of its 2003–2004 drug control budget spending to treatment and educating young people and communities. Only 38 percent to reducing the availability of drugs.

■ Former American President Ronald Reagan and his wife, Nancy, worked to reduce American drug abuse through Nancy's "Just Say No" campaign.

KEY CONCEPTS

Harrison Act Originally meant to be a registration law, the Harrison Act resulted in the arrests of thousands of physicians, pharmacists, and drug addicts. The act intended for doctors, pharmacists, and vendors would submit paperwork on all drug transactions, but the Treasury Department quickly used violations of the law to shut down legitimate practices as well as drug clinics and illicit drug stores. The Treasury Department assumed that any prescription for a narcotic given to a drug addict by a physician or pharmacist constituted conspiracy to violate the Harrison Act. Restricting the practice of medicine was not the original intent of the Harrison Act, but two 5–4 Supreme Court decisions held that the federal government could assume that a physician's prescription of a narcotic for the comfort or maintenance of an addict was a violation of the "good faith" practice of medicine, and therefore a criminal violation.

Medical Scientist

Duties: Research to understand the causes of and discover treatments for disease and other health problems
Education: Ph.D. in a biological science, medical degree (M.D.)
Interests: Chemistry, biology, solving problems

For information on careers in the biological sciences, click on **www.aibs.org** to visit the American Institute of Biological Sciences. Also navigate to **www.asm.org** for the American Society for Microbiology.

Careers in Focus

Biological scientists research ways to develop medicines, vaccines, and treatments for diseases. They are responsible for discovering how human genes work and how certain genes are associated with specific diseases or hereditary traits. Medical scientists are biological scientists who concentrate exclusively on biomedical research.

Medical scientists observe changes in a cell, chromosome, or gene that can signal the development of certain diseases. After identifying these changes, medical scientists research how to treat these medical problems. Medical scientists who have a medical degree can run clinical trials and test how different combinations of drugs and treatments work on a patient. They can then adjust the dosage or treatment to reduce negative side effects or to find better treatment results. Medical scientists also try to discover ways to prevent health problems from developing, such as affirming the link between smoking and lung cancer.

Many medical scientists work for corporations where their research is based on the company's needs. Other medical scientists depend on grant money to support their own research. There can be intense competition for grants.

A Ph.D. in biological science is the minimum education required to become a medical scientist. A Ph.D. qualifies a researcher to conduct research on particular medical problems or diseases, and analyze and interpret the results of experiments on patients. Medical scientists spend several years gaining laboratory experience, learning specific processes and techniques, before applying for permanent jobs.

Careers in Focus

Dictionary of Drugs

Drug	Common Street Name(s)	Derived From	Characteristics
alcohol	booze, sauce, juice	beverages based on ethanol	ingested; causes temporary dissociation, euphoria, and socialization
amphetamines	bennies, dexies, sparklers, pixies	misused prescription drugs and illicit varieties of prescription drugs	cause wakefulness, mental alertness, increased initiative and confidence, euphoria
barbiturates	barbs, downers, reds, blue devils, yellow jackets	derivatives of barbituric acid	used medically as sedatives or as an adjunct in anesthesia
benzedrine	bennies	chemical variant of amphetamine	euphoric stimulant effect
caffeine	upper, jolt, fix	found in coffee, tea, cocao, and some other plants	increases blood pressure, stimulates the central nervous system, promotes urine formation
cannabis	pot, grass, weed	dried leaves and flowers of the hemp plant	hallucinogenic that is smoked or chewed
cocaine	coke, snow, big c, Snow White	coca plant leaves	inhaled, smoked, or injected for mild euphoria, stimulation, and alertness
codeine	Empirin compound with codeine or Tylenol with codeine	naturally occurring alkaloid of opium; mostly produced from morphine	ingested or injected; used in medicine as a cough suppressant and narcotic analgesic drug
diazepam (valium)	V, downer	manufactured	relieves anxiety
flunitrazepam	date-rape drug, roofies	manufactured	produces sedative-hypnotic effects
hashish	hash, bhong, gram, quarter moon, soles	made of cannabis sativa resin only	hallucinogenic that is smoked or ingested; more potent than cannabis
heroin	smack, horse, junk, black tar, horse, train	derived from morphine	inhaled or injected; creates feelings of ecstasy when injected; produces drowsy state of relaxation and contentment

Drug	Common Street Name(s)	Derived From	Characteristics
lysergic acid diethylamide (LSD)	acid, blotter, dots, smears	synthesized from lysergic acid	evokes dreamlike changes in mood and thought, and alters perception of space and time
marijuana	pot, grass, weed	contains the dried flowers and leaves of the hemp plant	hallucinogenic that is smoked, chewed, or eaten
mescaline	mescal-button, half moon, mescal	from the peyote cactus	hallucinogenic
methamphetamine	crank, crystal, ice, speed, meth, cinnamon	produced by illicit laboratories	usually ingested as a pill or inhaled as a powder; increases physical activity; suppresses appetite
methylenedioxymeth amphetamine (MDMA)	Ecstasy, igloo, Tweety Birds, white diamonds	chemically related to amphetamines	designer drug, mood-enhancing, associated with rave culture
morphine	morf, dreamer, unkie	processed from opium	injected; used as a medical painkiller; produces a relaxed, drowsy state
nicotine (tobacco)	cigarettes, cigs, smokes, snuff, chew	dried tobacco leaves	inhaled through cigarettes, cigars, and pipes; stimulant
opium	big o, toxy, skee, zero	paste from opium poppy	smoked, eaten, or injected; painkilling properties; produces pleasure and euphoria
phencyclidine (PCP)	angel dust, hog, worm, mad dog	general anesthetic	hallucinogenic; alters time perception, sense of reality, and mood; induces dreamlike states
psilocybin	magic mushroom	from a particular type of mushroom	hallucinogenic; alters time perception, sense of reality, and mood; induces dreamlike states
Ritalin (brand name of methylphenidate)	Vitamin R, R-Ball, smart drug	synthetically produced	stimulant; improves attention and focus; calms hyperactive children

Dictionary of Drugs

Timeline of Events

1820
Caffeine is discovered in coffee.

1827
Theine is discovered in tea. It is not until 1838, however, that it is established that theine is identical to caffeine.

1839–1842
The first opium war between Great Britain and China occurs.

1856–1860
The second opium war between Great Britain and China occurs. Great Britain gains control over Hong Kong when the war ends.

1874
Heroin is first synthesized from morphine.

1903
Coca Cola™ discontinues use of cocaine in the Coca-Cola™ beverage.

1914
The Harrison Act is passed in the United States. This act bans recreational use of opium and cocaine.

1920
Prohibition begins in the United States at midnight on January 16.

1933
In December, Prohibition in the United States ends when liquor control returns to state governments.

1937
Medical use of marijuana is banned in the United States.

1938
Lysergic acid diethylamide (LSD) is discovered.

1964
The U.S. Surgeon General warns of the health dangers cigarettes pose.

1965
The use of phencyclidine (PCP) in humans is banned.

1971
U.S. President Richard Nixon declares a "war on drugs."

1973
The Drug Enforcement Agency (DEA) is created.

1981
The first conclusive evidence on the danger of passive smoking is revealed in Takeshi Hirayama's study on lung cancer in non-smoking Japanese women married to smokers.

1988
World No Tobacco Day is created by a World Health Assembly Resolution in 1988. This is one of only four UN-agency related world days.

1996
Congress passes the Drug-Induced Rape Prevention and Punishment Act of 1996 in October. This legislation increases federal penalties for use of any controlled substance to aid in sexual assault over concerns about the abuse of Rohypnol and other similar sedative-hypnotics.

▬▬ **Tobacco is a leading source of crop income in the state of Kentucky.**

1997
Hong Kong returns to China's control.

1998
The tobacco industry agrees to pay the 50 U.S. states about $250 billion over 25 years to compensate for the costs of treating tobacco-related illnesses.

2001
Canada becomes the first country to regulate the medical use of marijuana. The Canadian government grows and distributes medicinal marijuana to screened applicants.

2002
A national survey determines that 14.4 percent of Americans—33.9 million people—have tried cocaine at least once. Two million people report using cocaine in the past month.

2003
The National Drug Intelligence Center issues a report stating cocaine is the primary drug threat in the United States because of its high demand and availability, expanding distribution to new markets, high rate of overdose, and relation to violence.

2004
In February, Great Britain reclassifies cannabis from Class B to Class C.

2005
About 30 percent of the world's general adult population uses tobacco and about half uses alcohol.

2006
The ban on smoking in public places, such as bars and restaurants, comes into effect in Scotland.

Concept Web

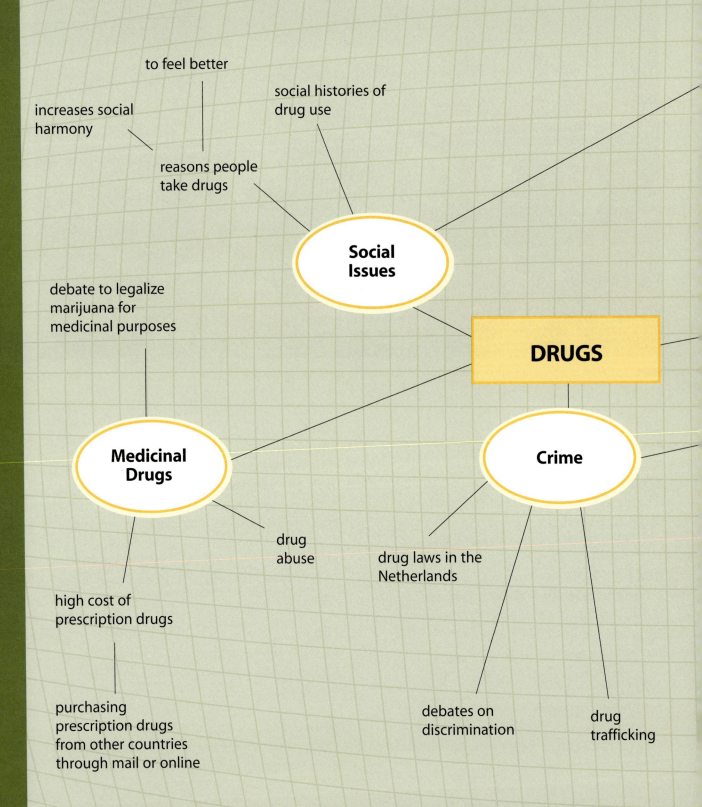

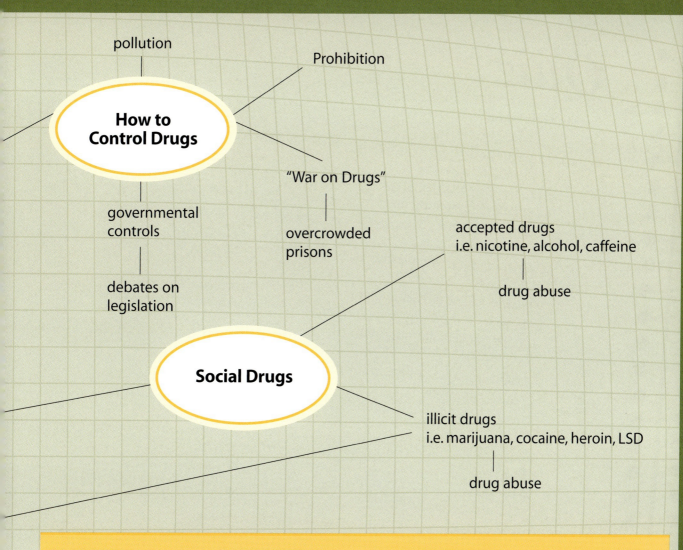

MAKE YOUR OWN CONCEPT WEB

A concept web is a useful summary tool. It can also be used to plan your research or help you write an essay or report. To make your own concept web, follow the steps below:

- You will need a large piece of unlined paper and a pencil.
- First, read through your source material, such as *Substance Use And Abuse* in the Understanding Global Issues series.
- Write the main idea, or concept, in large letters in the center of the page.
- On a sheet of lined paper, jot down all words, phrases, or lists that you know are connected with the concept. Try to do this from memory.
- Look at your list. Can you group your words and phrases in certain topics or themes? Connect the different topics with lines to the center, or to other "branches."
- Critique your concept web. Ask questions about the material on your concept web: Does it all make sense? Are all the links shown? Could there be other ways of looking at it? Is anything missing?
- What more do you need to find out? Develop questions for those areas you are still unsure about or where information is missing. Use these questions as a basis for further research.

Quiz

Multiple Choice

1. People take drugs for which of the following reasons:
    a) to enhance pleasure
    b) to improve performance
    c) to ease pain or ailments
    d) all of the above

2. Cannabis and marijuana are:
    a) the same.
    b) derived from the hemp plant.
    c) both from the hemp plant but cannabis is eaten and marijuana is smoked.
    d) both smoked, but not eaten.

3. Cocaine has which of the following medical uses?
    a) cough suppressant
    b) remedy for diarrhea and stomachache
    c) local anesthetic
    d) painkiller

4. What percent of regular smokers are addicted to nicotine?
    a) nicotine is not addictive
    b) 50 percent
    c) 30 percent
    d) 80 percent

5. How many injections do heroin addicts typically need each day to avoid withdrawal symptoms?
    a) one
    b) two
    c) three
    d) it depends on the addict

6. Caffeine affects the body by:
   a) decreasing urine output
   b) making users crave nicotine
   c) suppressing appetite
   d) stimulating the brain and heart, and increasing urine output

7. Which of the following methods delivers drugs to the brain fastest?
   a) eating or drinking
   b) intravenous injection
   c) inhalation
   d) sniffing up the nose

Where Did It Happen?

1. This was the first country in the world to regulate the medical use of marijuana.
2. These two countries fought the Opium Wars.
3. In 1917, this country made the production and sale of alcohol illegal.
4. This country accounts for 70 percent of coca grown in the world.

True or False

1. Heroin is the most frequently used illegal drug in the United States.
2. Tobacco is the most damaging drug humans use.
3. Marijuana use is legal in the Netherlands.
4. Cocaine is an ingredient in Coca-Cola™.

Answers on page 53

Internet Resources

The following websites provide more information on drugs:

NIDA
www.drugabuse.gov
Established in 1974, the National Institute on Drug Abuse (NIDA) supports more than 85 percent of world research on the health aspects of drug abuse and addiction. NIDA's goal is to ensure that science directs America's drug abuse reduction efforts. This site provides information fact sheets for commonly abused drugs, information for teenagers, parents, teachers, and researchers.

WHO
www.who.int/substance_abuse/en
Since its establishment in 1946, the World Health Organization (WHO) has attempted to aid individuals in every country to obtain the goal of health. The Management of Substance Dependence home page contains information about substance use and abuse. WHO is the only agency that deals with all psychoactive substances, regardless of their legal status.

Some websites stay current longer than others. To find other drug websites, enter terms such as "drug abuse," "marijuana," or "prescription drugs" into a search engine.

Further Reading

Carson-Dewitt, Rosalyn, editor. *Drugs, Alcohol, and Tobacco: Learning About Addictive Behavior.* New York: MacMillan Library Reference, 2004.

Lawler, Jennifer. *Drug Legalization: A Pro/Con Issue.* Berkeley Heights, NJ: Enslow Publishers, Inc., 1999.

Sheen, Barbara. *Teen Alcoholism.* San Diego, CA: Lucent Books, 2004.

Thomas, Gareth. *This is Ecstasy.* London, England: Sanctuary Publishing, 2004.

World Health Organization. *The Tobacco Atlas,* 2002.

Answers

Multiple Choice
1. d) 2. b) 3. c) 4. d) 5. b) 6. d) 7. c)

Where Did It Happen?
1. Canada 2. China and Great Britain 3. the United States 4. Colombia

True or False
1. F 2. T 3. F 4. F

Glossary

adulterated: to make impure by adding inferior ingredients

amphetamines: bitter-tasting liquid synthetic drugs that have a strong stimulating effect on the central nervous system

barbiturates: a class of organic compounds used in medicine as sedatives, hypnotics, or an adjunct in anesthesia

benzodiazepines: minor tranquilizer compound used as a short-term treatment for sleeping difficulties

black market: a system of illegally buying and selling officially controlled goods

bootleggers: people who transport and/or sell illegal goods

cannabis: the dried flowering tops of the female hemp plant

developed world: countries in the industrialized world; highly economically and technologically developed

developing world: those countries that are undergoing the process of industrialization

distillation: the process of separating, concentrating, or purifying liquid by boiling it and condensing the resulting vapor

excise taxes: taxes on goods for a domestic market

guerrilla: a soldier, usually with a political objective, such as the overthrow of a government

hypodermic syringe: an instrument consisting of a thin hollow needle attached to a small tube that is used to inject medicine or drugs under the skin or to withdraw fluids, especially blood, from under the skin

pharmaceutical: involved in or associated with the manufacture, preparation, dispensing, or sale of medical drugs

physiology: the organic processes and functions in an organism and/or its parts

Prohibition: the legal ban on the manufacture and sale of intoxicating beverages in the United States, lasting from 1920–1933

psychoactive drugs: chemical substances that alter mood, behavior, perception, or mental functioning

resin: a solid or semisolid natural organic substance secreted in the sap of some plants and trees that has a transparent or translucent quality and a yellow or brown color

serotonin receptors: proteins that sit on the surface of neurons (nerve cells) and bind serotonin, a chemical that constricts blood vessels at injury sites, and may affect emotional states

trafficking: buying and selling illegal drugs

water pipe: a pipe for smoking that is filled with water to cool the smoke by drawing it through the water

Index

addiction 5, 10, 13, 14, 15, 16, 23, 24, 31, 33, 34, 39
Afghanistan 16. 30, 32
alcohol 5, 6, 8, 9, 13, 15, 16, 18, 20, 30, 31, 35, 37, 39, 44, 47, 49
amphetamines 5, 7, 11, 16, 18, 24, 28, 31, 33, 39, 41, 44, 45
anesthetic 13, 25, 45
antidepressants 14
Asia 10, 14, 23, 28, 29, 31, 32, 33

barbiturates 5, 13, 41, 44
black market 11, 32, 33, 39
brain 5, 7, 15, 16, 18, 23, 25

caffeine 6, 16, 18, 19, 44, 46, 49
cannabis 5, 6, 10, 13, 15, 22, 23, 29, 31, 33, 34, 35, 39, 40, 41, 44, 47
China 8, 9, 11, 32, 46
Coca-Cola™ 10, 46
cocaine 5, 6, 9, 10, 13, 18, 19, 22, 23, 25, 28, 29, 30, 33, 34, 35, 39, 40, 41, 44, 46, 47, 49
codeine 5, 10, 13, 44
Colombia 30, 33, 41
crack 23, 34, 39, 40
crime 5, 27, 28, 32, 34, 35, 39, 41, 49

delta-9-tetrahydrocannabinol (THC) 22, 23
depressants 13, 16

Europe 8, 9, 10, 14, 15, 18, 20, 29, 31, 36, 40

Great Britain 5, 10, 15, 18, 19, 22, 25, 34, 42, 46, 47

hallucinogens 13, 16, 25, 41, 44, 45
Harrison Act 39, 42, 46
hashish 8, 23, 29, 44
hemp 8, 10, 15, 22, 39, 40, 44, 45
heroin 5, 11, 13, 16, 18, 19, 23, 24, 32, 33, 34, 35, 39, 41, 44, 46, 49

India 8, 15, 20, 22

legalization 35, 41, 42
Lysergic Acid Diethylamide (LSD) 5, 7, 10, 11, 16, 25, 28, 40, 44, 46, 49

marijuana 5, 7, 10, 15, 22, 23, 26, 35, 40, 41, 45, 46, 47
methylenedioxymethamphetamine (MDMA) 6, 7, 11, 25, 33, 34, 45
Mexico 33
morphine 5, 9, 10, 13, 16, 23, 44, 45, 46

Netherlands 33, 35, 41, 48
nicotine 5, 6, 7, 14, 19, 45, 49

opiates 13, 16, 22, 26, 28, 28, 29, 34
opium 8, 9, 10, 11, 13, 16, 23, 26, 32, 33, 36, 39, 41, 44, 45, 46

phencyclidine (PCP) 25, 45, 46
prescription drugs 13, 14, 17, 30, 42, 44, 48
Prohibition 5, 6, 7, 14, 19, 46, 49

Russia 8, 11, 33

sleep 18, 24
sleeping pills 13, 16
stimulants 13, 16, 18, 23, 24, 28, 29, 33, 44, 45
synthetic drugs 5, 9, 22, 41, 45

taxes 8, 20, 39, 41
tobacco 5, 8, 19, 20, 21, 30, 37, 45, 46, 47

United Nations (UN) 5, 22, 24, 28, 32, 33, 41, 46

Vietnam 11, 32

war on drugs 23, 40, 41, 46

Credits

All of the Internet URLs given in the book were valid at the time of publication. However, due to the dynamic nature of the Internet, some addresses may have changed, or sites may have ceased to exist since publication. While the author and publisher regret any inconvenience this may cause readers, no responsibility for any such changes can be accepted by either the author or the publisher.

Every reasonable effort has been made to trace ownership and to obtain permission to reprint copyright material. The publishers would be pleased to have any errors or omissions brought to their attention so that they may be corrected in subsequent printings.